This book belongs to

Tyler

Published by Scholastic Inc., 90 Old Sherman Turnpike, Danbury, Connecticut 06816.

ISBN: 0-439-87929-9

Printed in the U.S.A.

First Scholastic printing, November 2006

The Halfhearted Viking

A Lesson in
Doing Your Best

by **Doug Peterson**
Illustrated by **Warner McGee**

SCHOLASTIC INC.

New York Toronto London Auckland Sydney
Mexico City New Delhi Hong Kong Buenos Aires

Even Vikings need a vacation. And one of the favorite Viking vacation spots was the Pillage Inn Resort on the coast of Denmark.

"Say cheese!" Sven shouted, snapping a group photo by the pool. A huge sign greeted them that read "Have a Plunderful Time at the Pillage Inn."

It was as perfect as a postcard—until the monster showed up.

Have a
Plunderful Time
at the **Pillage Inn**

Well, actually, things started going wrong even before the monster came along. It all went downhill the moment the Vikings met the hotel owner, Halfdanish, and his little dog, Beo-Woof.

Halfdanish was a Viking, too. But he was a halfhearted Viking. He never put his whole heart into anything. He never did his best, especially when it came to running the hotel.

Halfdanish carried their suitcases only halfway to their rooms and then dropped them on the floor. "It's the best I can do," he said.

Even more shocking, the hotel room was half the size of a

normal room, and the beds were half the size of normal beds.

"I thought we were getting king-sized beds," said Olaf.

"Sorry. We only have peasant-sized beds," said Halfdanish.

"It's the best I can do."

Every day, the maids cleaned
only half of the room.

The restaurant served
half-cooked meals. And the
waiters spilled half of the
food on the Vikings.

The Vikings tried their best to enjoy themselves anyway. During their first hour at the Pillage Inn, Sven had already taken 1,214 photos.

But when Ottar and Sven found out that their hotel towels were only half-dry, it was time to complain. They went straight to the front desk.

"In addition to the half-dry towels, the TV in our room only shows half of a picture," griped Ottar.

"Sorry, it's the best I can do," Halfdanish said. He shrugged and went back to reading the newspaper.

"Is this really the best you can do?" asked Ottar. "God asks us to serve others with *all* of our heart. When you put all of your heart into something and do your best, it shows that you care. But you don't care about anyone but yourself!"

Halfdanish looked up from his paper and said, "Sorry. What was that you said? I was only half listening."

Ottar let out a groan.

"Here's the deal," added Halfdanish, setting down the paper. "I'll give you guys bigger rooms if you do a little something for me."

"What little something?" Ottar asked. He didn't like the sound of this.

"Just get rid of a little pest in our hotel," said Halfdanish.

"You mean bugs?" asked Sven.

"No, a monster," said Halfdanish. "Get rid of our monster problem, and I'll give you a bigger room."

Ottar and Sven were shocked.

"You must be half crazy if you think we're going to fight a monster for you!" Ottar shouted.

"I'll also give you half price on your room," Halfdanish bargained.

"It's a deal," said Ottar.

So that very night, Ottar and Sven hid in the storage room next to the kitchen.

"Halfdanish said the monster broke into the hotel last night and took lots of hotel towels," Ottar told Sven.

"The horror!" Sven exclaimed. "What kind of beast are we dealing with? What kind of monster would take a hotel towel? What kind of—"

"Sshhhhhhh," cried Ottar. "Did you hear that?"

"You mean the sound of me talking?" whispered Sven. "When I talk, I always hear myself. That's the way it usually works."

"No. *That*," said Ottar.

There it was—the sound of a door creaking open. Something had entered the kitchen—something breathing very, very hard.

Ottar peeked through the door.
The shadow of a hideous beast was cast
against the kitchen wall. The monster had
huge spiky horns and a long pointy tail!

"Are you ready?" whispered Ottar.

"Ready," said Sven, trembling.

"Now!" Ottar said.

The two brave Vikings barged into the kitchen.

The flash of Sven's camera lit up the dark room like lightning. Ottar hurled his net over the horrible creature.

With Ottar on the monster's back, it thrashed and bashed through the kitchen like a clumsy bull on a waxed floor in a china shop. Pots and pans crashed and dishes broke.

Finally, the creature tumbled to
the floor, wrapped up in the net.

CLICK!

Someone turned on the light in the kitchen.

It was Halfdanish, still in his pajamas.

"I was half asleep when I heard the ruckus," said Halfdanish.

"Did you capture the monster?"

"We sure did!" declared Ottar proudly.

"Behold the beast!" Ottar stepped aside to see what kind of monster

he had caught. It was terrifying. It was horrible. It was—

"Norse and Rune?" Halfdanish exclaimed. "What are you doing in the kitchen?"

"Where's the monster?" asked Sven. "We saw a hideous creature with horns

and a spiked tail!"

"Don't you see, Sven," said Ottar. "They **are** the monster! And look, they're stealing towels again."

"You're fired!" shouted Halfdanish.

"No! Wait!" Sven said. "They're not *stealing* the towels. I think they're bringing them back—fluffy clean and lemony fresh!"

"Your employees really care," came a voice from the door. It was the guy from the all-night laundry place. "Norse and Rune weren't happy with half-dry towels in this hotel. So they've been bringing them to me in the middle of the night."

Halfdanish was stunned. "I didn't know how much you cared about this hotel," he said to his two employees.

"They care and do their very best. They're no monster," said the laundry guy.

And that's when it happened. Some how, some way, Halfdanish's heart became whole that night. Norse and Rune had shown him how wonderful it was to put your whole heart into something.

From that moment on, things changed at the Pillage Inn. Halfdanish made sure the meals were fully cooked, the beds were fully made, and room service employees brought meals all the way to the room.

But best of all, Halfdanish found out that doing his best made him not half happy—but totally happy.

And that isn't half bad.

Dear Aunt Hilde,
Having a plunderful time in Denmark.
Wish you were here. With all my heart, — Sven

Work at everything you do with all your heart.
Work as if you were working for the Lord,
not for human masters.
Colossians 3:23